Engineer Ari
and the
Passover Rush

By Deborah Bodin Cohen
illustrations by Shahar Kober

KAR-BEN
PUBLISHING

The Story of Passover

The first Passover happened long ago in the far-away country of Egypt. A mean and powerful king, called Pharaoh, ruled Egypt. Worried that the Jewish people would one day fight against him, Pharaoh decided that these people must become his slaves. As slaves, the Jewish people worked very hard. Every day, from morning until night, they hammered, dug, and carried heavy bricks. They built palaces and cities and worked without rest. The Jewish people hated being slaves. They cried and asked God for help. God chose a man named Moses to lead the Jewish people. Moses went to Pharaoh and said, "God is not happy with the way you treat the Jewish people. He wants you to let the Jewish people leave Egypt and go into the desert, where they will be free." But Pharaoh stamped his foot and shouted, "No, I will never let the Jewish people go!" Moses warned, "If you do not listen to God, many terrible things, called plagues, will come to your land." But Pharaoh would not listen, and so the plagues arrived. First, the water turned to blood. Next, frogs and, later, wild animals ran in and out of homes. Balls of hail fell from the sky and bugs, called locusts, ate all of the Egyptians' food.

Each time a new plague began, Pharaoh would cry, "Moses, I'll let the Jewish people go. Just stop this horrible plague!" Yet no sooner would God take away the plague than Pharaoh would shout: "No, I've changed my mind. The Jews must stay!" So God sent more plagues. Finally, as the tenth plague arrived, Pharaoh ordered the Jews to leave Egypt.

Fearful that Pharaoh might again change his mind, the Jewish people packed quickly. They had no time to prepare food and no time to allow their dough to rise into puffy bread. They had only enough time to make a flat, cracker-like bread called matzah. They hastily tied the matzah to their backs and ran from their homes.

The people had not travelled far before Pharaoh commanded his army to chase after them and bring them back to Egypt. The Jews dashed forward, but stopped when they reached a large sea. The sea was too big to swim across. Frightened that Pharaoh's men would soon reach them, the people prayed to God, and a miracle occurred. The sea opened up. Two walls of water stood in front of them and a dry, sandy path stretched between the walls. The Jews ran across. Just as they reached the other side, the walls of water fell and the path disappeared. The sea now separated the Jews from the land of Egypt. They were free!

Each year at Passover, we eat special foods, sing songs, tell stories, and participate in a *seder* — a special meal designed to help us remember this miraculous journey from slavery to freedom.

For Ezra Matan, whose smile and laughter brightens our seder table—D.B.C

KAR-BEN PUBLISHING
An imprint of Lerner Publishing Group, Inc.
241 First Avenue North
Minneapolis, MN 55401 USA
1-800-4-Karben

Website address: www.karben.com

Main body text set in BernhardGothic Medium.
Typeface provided by The Font Company.

Library of Congress Cataloging-in-Publication Data

Cohen, Deborah Bodin, 1968–
    Engineer Ari and the Passover rush / by Deborah Bodin Cohen ; illustrated by Shahar Kober.
        pages   cm.
    Summary: "In 1893, Engineer Ari is in a rush to get his train to Jerusalem and back before Passover, and he still needs many things for his seder plate. Luckily he has many friends to help" — Provided by publisher.
        ISBN 978-1-4677-3470-7 (lib. bdg. : alk. paper)
    [1. Passover—Fiction. 2. Seder—Fiction. 3. Railroad trains—Fiction.] I. Kober, Shahar, illustrator. II. Title.
PZ7.C6623Emp 2015
[E]—dc23   2014003601

Manufactured in China
1-50825-50164-7/30/2021

0322/B1852/A4

"**Cock-a-doodle-doo**," crowed the rooster. Engineer Ari opened his eyes and yawned. He looked at his pocket watch and jumped out of bed.

There was only one more day until the Passover seder with his engineer friends, Jessie and Nathaniel. And before then, Engineer Ari had to drive one last train to Jerusalem and back. He dressed quickly and left the house, taking long, quick strides towards Jaffa's train station.

Engineer Ari had tucked a seder shopping list into his pocket: roasted egg, charoset, parsley, horseradish, shankbone, matzah. But the spring air was sweet, and he didn't want to rush. As he bent down to pick a flower, his watch fell on the ground and reminded him of the passing time. I better not dawdle, he sighed.

Engineer Ari passed the house of his neighbor Miriam. She was chasing a hen around her courtyard. "*Boker Tov*, good morning!" he called. "Your rooster woke me up this morning!"

"Ari, take a fresh egg for your seder plate," said Miriam.

"I am in a rush," said Engineer Ari. "I don't have time to take it home."

"Then I'll roast the egg and leave it on your doorstep," said Miriam.

Engineer Ari hurried down a footpath through a small orchard of date palms. Ahead, he saw a ladder and two legs disappearing into a tree. "Is that you, Moshe?" he called.

A man in dungarees and a lopsided turban jumped down. "Shalom, Ari," said Moshe, holding up a bunch of dates. "I'm picking fruit for my grandmother's charoset. Care to join me? I'm off to pick almonds next."

"So sorry. I've got a train schedule to keep," said Engineer Ari. "But, your grandmother's charoset does sound delicious."

"Stop by on your way home," said Moshe. "I'll make extra for your seder plate."

"*Todah rabah*, Moshe," said Engineer Ari. "And, I'll bring you matzah from Jerusalem."

He crossed "charoset" off his list.

Engineer Ari dashed into the railway station. The train was already full of passengers. In no time, he pushed the throttle, and the train steamed out of the station. Engineer Ari pulled the whistle cord,

"Toot, Toot."

The train **CHUG-A-LUGGED** through a valley of wild flowers. Engineer Ari saw his friend Shifra waving from her garden.

"*Rega, rega,* wait, wait," called Shifra.

Engineer Ari stepped on the brakes. "Shalom, Shifra!" he called. "I'm in a hurry. I'm making one last trip to Jerusalem before Passover!"

"That is why I stopped you," said Shifra. "I have too much parsley. Would you like some for your seder plate?"

She handed him a bunch of parsley from her basket.

"*Todah rabah,* Shifra," he said. "I'll leave a box of matzah for you on my way back." He crossed "parsley" off his list.

At the next station, Engineer Ari's friend Aaron was waiting. His face was bright red and grimacing.

Ari looked at his pocket watch. "Are you angry that I am late?" he asked.

"I am not angry," sputtered Aaron, holding up a large root. "I tasted the horseradish. It is very spicy!"

"Drink some water!" said Engineer Ari, handing him a canteen.

Aaron took a long drink. "I don't need so much horseradish," he said, breaking the root in half. "Here's some for your seder plate."

"*Todah rabah*, Aaron," said Engineer Ari. "I'll stop back on my way home and leave a box of matzah for you." He crossed "horseradish" off his list.

Engineer Ari **CHUG-A-LUGGED** into the Jerusalem station.
He pulled the whistle cord,

"Toot, Toot."

He looked at his pocket watch. If he hurried, he could finish his errands before the train was scheduled to return to Jaffa.

Ari hustled through the Old City. First he picked up a shankbone at the butcher. Then he went to the matzah factory.

Matzah Factory
KOSHER

Inside, the workers were rushing about.

One mixed the dough,

another rolled it out,

a third poked holes in it,

A woman with a pocket watch
kept track of the time.

and still another hurried to
put it into the oven.

"Why are you working so quickly?" asked Engineer Ari.

"We must hurry," answered Batya the baker. "We have only 18 minutes to make the matzah.

"18 minutes?" said Ari. "That is more rushed than *my* schedule!"

"Any longer and the matzah might rise like bread," said Batya. "Just as the Israelites hurried to leave Egypt, we hurry to make our matzah."

"Like you, I am in a rush. I have a train schedule to keep," said Engineer Ari. "But I need matzah for my seder and some for my friends."

Batya sold him five boxes of matzah.
"*Todah rabah*, Batya," said Engineer Ari.

Ari crossed "matzah" off his list. Now he had everything.

On his way back, Engineer Ari made quick stops to drop off boxes of matzah for Shifra and Aaron.

And right on schedule, he steamed into Jaffa station.

He stopped by Moshe's house and traded matzah for charoset.

Then he visited Miriam and gave her matzah, too.

Home at last, an exhausted Engineer Ari opened the door. His friends, Jessie and Nathaniel, were setting the seder table. Pillows were placed on the chairs, so everybody could recline and relax during the seder.

Engineer Ari unpacked everything that he had collected. "Sit down and rest a little," said Nathaniel. "Jessie and I will get the seder plate ready."

"Thank you," said Ari. "I am so tired from rushing."

A few minutes later, Jessie and Nathaniel came into the dining room. Jessie carried the silver seder plate with the egg, charoset, parsley, horseradish, and shankbone on it. Nathaniel carried the platter of matzah with its embroidered cover.

"*Chag sameach*, Ari," said Jessie.

"Happy holiday," said Nathaniel. "It's time for our seder to begin!"

But Engineer Ari just let out a loud snore.

Author's Note

On August 27, 1892, the first train steamed into Jerusalem from Jaffa, carrying passengers and cargo. A month later, during the High Holidays, the railway officially opened. The train shortened the trip between the Mediterranean coast and Jerusalem from 3 days to 3½ hours. Eliezer Ben-Yehuda, the father of modern Hebrew, who lived in Jerusalem at the time, coined the word *rakevet* (train) from the Biblical word for "chariot."

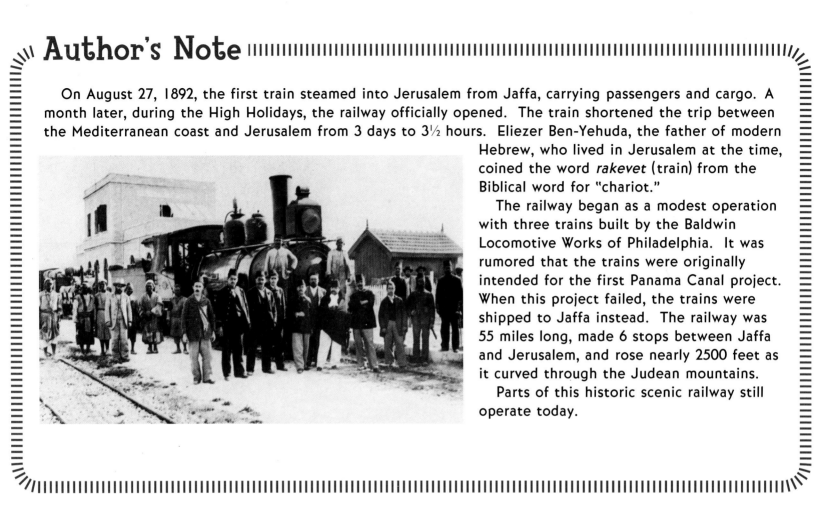

The railway began as a modest operation with three trains built by the Baldwin Locomotive Works of Philadelphia. It was rumored that the trains were originally intended for the first Panama Canal project. When this project failed, the trains were shipped to Jaffa instead. The railway was 55 miles long, made 6 stops between Jaffa and Jerusalem, and rose nearly 2500 feet as it curved through the Judean mountains.

Parts of this historic scenic railway still operate today.

GLOSSARY

Charoset – a dish of chopped apples and walnuts that is eaten on Passover to remind us of the mortar used by the Israelites to make bricks for Pharaoh

Todah rabah – Hebrew for "thank you very much"

Rega – literally Hebrew for a "second," but is used to mean "wait a second" or "wait"

Chag sameach – Hebrew for the greeting "Happy Holiday!"